I0458151

LOVE LIKE BLUE

Kristen Lazarian

Queen of Wands Publishing

LOVE LIKE BLUE

was first produced at the Whitefire Theatre
in Sherman Oaks, California

ISBN 978-0-578-10137-8

Please note the following:

- No one shall commit or authorize any act of addition or omission by which the copyright of, or the right to copyright, this play may be impaired.

- No one shall make any changes in this play for purposes of production.

- Publication of this play does not imply availability of performance. Both amateurs and professionals who would like to produce this play are advised to apply for written permission before starting rehearsals, advertising or booking a theatre.

- No part of this book may be reproduced, stored in a retrieval system, or transmitted in any form, by any means, now known or yet to be invented, including mechanical, electronic, photocopying, recording, videotaping, or otherwise, without prior consent of the publisher.

Credit Requirements:

Producers of **LOVE LIKE BLUE** must give credit to the Author of the Play in all programs and all publicity materials distributed in connection with performances of the Play, and in all instances in which the title of the Play appears for the purposes of advertising, publicity, or otherwise exploiting the Play and production. The name of the Author must appear on a separate line on which no other name appears, immediately following the title and must appear in size of type not less than fifty percent of the size of the title type. The Author must not have name in type smaller than that of the Director.

Characters

CARISSA an artist, 30's

SARAH   an attorney, 30's-40's

WYNNE a student, a waif, 20ish

NOLAN an accountant, married to Sarah, 40's

FELIX an author, 30's-40's (*same age as Sarah*)

EDDIE an art history professor, 30's

Settings

ACT ONE

> **Scene One** The studio
>
> **Scene Two** The dining room
>
> **Scene Three** The study

ACT TWO

> **Scene One** The study
>
> **Scene Two** The dining room
>
> **Scene Three** The studio

Time

The Present.

Act One

that same sad, strange,
and darkest night
when love fades away

ACT ONE - SCENE ONE
"CARISSA & EDDIE"

The interior of Carissa's art studio/loft.

At open, Carissa paints. She is reckless with her brush soaked in blue, stroking an enormous canvas that dwarfs her. She works aimlessly as if she's painting her rage and nothing else.

She's alone. Tarps are scattered on the floor. A portable music player sits Upstage Right. Driving rock music plays loudly, very loudly.

Eddie, a conservative looking man in his thirties, enters unnoticed with a box of Chinese take-out. He takes an occasional bite as he watches Carissa paint.

He is wet. He has just come in from the rain.

EDDIE. You see your therapist today?

Carissa doesn't hear him. She's in full flow, painting.

EDDIE. Did you see your therapist today?!

Frustrated, Eddie goes over to the stereo and turns off the music. Carissa, jolted, SCREAMS.

EDDIE. Are you done?

CARISSA. What the fuck are you doing? How many times have I explained to you that I can't be interrupted when I'm working? You come in here and you—it's like I'm having the best sex dream of my life and then having the phone ring right when I'm about to have an orgasm. I wake up and it's ruined.

EDDIE. Hungry?

CARISSA. Fuck off.

Carissa paints, turning her back on Eddie.

EDDIE. You've been here for four days. I thought you might be hungry.

CARISSA. I'm not. I'm not hungry.

EDDIE. Did you see that guy you see?

CARISSA. What guy?

EDDIE. What guy. Your therapist. Did you see him?

CARISSA. What does it matter if I did or not?

EDDIE. It matters because normally you see him on Tuesdays. It's Tuesday night.

CARISSA. No, it's—

EDDIE. Yes, Carissa. It is. It's after nine o'clock. If you looked outside you'd see it's dark. You'd see it's dark and the movie you were supposed to meet me at had already started somewhere around two hours ago.

CARISSA. No, I didn't see Dr. Nod.

EDDIE. Nod? That's the guy's name?

CARISSA. I can't pronounce his name. It's Polish.

EDDIE. You didn't see him?

CARISSA. Who the fuck cares either way.

EDDIE. I care.

CARISSA. Since when, Eddie. Please.

EDDIE. Since right now. I can't figure out what he does for you.

CARISSA. Well, he has a thick gray beard and black—jet black eyebrows and piercing blue eyes. Ice blue like the color of love. And he purrs before he makes complete sentences that half the time I can't understand because his accent's so thick but the sound—the sound of his voice makes me quiver. And he usually sits with his hands folded across the top of his chest—like this—and he nods at me before I answer questions. Then he nods again when I give him stupid fucking explanations for things in my life I don't really understand at all.

EDDIE. Is that all?

CARISSA. And he's always interested in how I feel and he nurtures my creative life and he knows my secrets. Not to mention the fact that he's gentle and reassuring and usually when I'm driving home after a session with him, all I can think about is how nice it would be to sleep with him.

EDDIE. Did you call him and tell him you couldn't make it today or did you just not show up?

CARISSA. Technicalities.

EDDIE. Common courtesy is not a technicality.

CARISSA. It's not a necessity.

EDDIE. It just seems to me that your shrink would be upset if you didn't show up for your appointment.

CARISSA. I don't care.

EDDIE. You're isolating.

CARISSA. I'm working. I work alone. I can concentrate better that way. Now, if you'll excuse me—

EDDIE. I won't excuse you. Not this time, not the next time.

CARISSA. It's not that big of a deal. I planned on going. I got in my car and then it dawned on me that this painting needed blue and it was all I kept thinking about—blue, blue, blue— and so I came back up here—see—

Carissa holds up a wet paint brush, dripping with blue.

Blue.

Beat. She goes back to the painting.

He makes it worse anyway—this problem I have to think myself into knots. One thought—and it mutates in a thousand different directions and I feel like a failure if I don't follow each twisted little version of that original thought until I am so fucking confused I don't know what I was thinking in the first place. And somewhere I forget what's right and wrong or how I even feel and it all becomes a game. Me trying to get out of this web in my mind. That's the game I play almost every day and always as I'm trying to fall asleep. This is the only thing that's keeping me from losing it completely. This, right here. This one painting is what saves me. Next week, next month it might be a different painting. But right now, at this moment in my life, I need this painting—and so, yes, it is more important to me than you or Nod or anything because I am barely hanging on as it is.

EDDIE. People need you, Carissa. You need people. That's how we're meant to be—as human beings. We're meant to live by relating to each other. Even Emily Dickinson wrote letters.

Beat. Carissa glares at Eddie.

You need people—you need me to walk into this room, to feed you, for God's sake, to look at what you've done and to tell you it's beautiful or that it touches me or that you're brilliant. And if you're gonna tell me that's not true, you're a—

CARISSA. It is true. Except that's never what you say to me. You come in here and you turn off my music and you interrupt me and then you look at my work and don't say anything at all or you tell me that the color's wrong or that it doesn't make sense. That's not what I need from you.

Eddie moves behind Carissa, looking at her canvas.

EDDIE. You're expression isn't the only one that counts.
CARISSA. Express whatever you want but stay the fuck away from me and my work. Because, Eddie—Eddie, you don't really know anything about what this takes.
EDDIE. It takes you away from me! That's what it takes!
CARISSA. You're jealous.

Eddie paces behind Carissa. He looks at the canvas from different angles.

Don't stand there and scrutinize. It pisses me off.

EDDIE. At least I'm provoking some sort of emotional response.
CARISSA. Fuck you! (*Calmly*) Can you identify that emotion?

Eddie comes down to Carissa and moves the hair off the back of her neck.

EDDIE. I had a dream last night that you were masturbating with a paintbrush in front of your therapist.

Carissa laughs.

I'd say that's worth analyzing.

CARISSA. Sounds pretty simplistic to me.
EDDIE. Explain it to me then.

CARISSA. I'm always explaining things to you.

Eddie kisses her neck.

EDDIE. Let's have sex.
CARISSA. I'm trying to work.
EDDIE. You tell me I'm not spontaneous so I'm being spontaneous.
CARISSA. You want to distract me.
EDDIE. I want some of your attention.
CARISSA. I'm giving you my attention.
EDDIE. I want more. I want you to put down the brush and I want
        you to engage in me. I want intimacy. I want you to talk to
        me—

Carissa laughs.

Or we can just fuck and you can think of your shrink's ice blue
eyes.

CARISSA. I've done that already.
EDDIE. I think I stay in this relationship because I have deep seated
        hatred toward myself.
CARISSA. Here we go—
EDDIE. You wanna know what hurts, Carissa?
CARISSA. Is this vulnerability? I'm shocked.
EDDIE. It hurts to walk in here and see you engrossed in a painting
        when I've been waiting in the rain for tickets to a Bergman film
        you wanted to see and that I don't give a damn about.
CARISSA. So we didn't go. Calm down.
EDDIE. We didn't go because you're here.
CARISSA. You're making me crazy. I think you should leave.
EDDIE. I'm making you crazy?
CARISSA. I'm trying to work.
EDDIE. And I'm trying to have a relationship with you!

CARISSA. Stop trying! This shouldn't be so fucking difficult.

>*Beat.*

No—come here.

EDDIE. No.

CARISSA. Come on. Come here.

EDDIE. Why?

CARISSA. So we can do it. I thought you wanted to.

EDDIE. It's not spontaneous anymore.

CARISSA. It wasn't spontaneous to begin with. It's not spontaneous to say—let's have sex. It's spontaneous to just let it happen. To kiss me once like it's just a kiss, you know, but then to realize how good it feels and then to kiss me again, longer, until the blood starts rushing down there and all you can think about is how good it would be to get naked and sweaty. And it doesn't matter who's around or how bad the timing is because the most important thing in the whole world is the moment and the sensation and—

EDDIE. Right. And then the phone rings.

CARISSA. Or you say something stupid like that.

EDDIE. I'm sorry. I'm sorry that everything that comes out of my mouth isn't poetry.

CARISSA. I don't want poetry—one profound sentence might be refreshing but I've learned to live without that.

EDDIE. Ice blue eyes like the color of love? What the hell is that?

CARISSA. Love takes on different shades of blue at different stages. But most of the time it's ice blue.

EDDIE. Love is not blue.

CARISSA. It's not red.

EDDIE. I didn't say it was red.

CARISSA. It just seems like you're the type who would think love is red. Most people do. But, I'm sorry, love is very rarely red.

EDDIE. You think I'm that predictable that I would say love is red?

CARISSA. Yeah, actually I do.

EDDIE. I think love is transparent.

CARISSA. That's impossible. I mean, maybe you can see through it every now and then but it's never perfectly clear. It's always got a shade to it.

EDDIE. Not from my view. Not the kind of love I want.

CARISSA. Love like that would be too simple. There'd be no mystery, nothing to question. No. Love has a color and usually it's some kind of blue.

EDDIE. Once again, Carissa has all the answers. This one, however, deserves a Nobel Prize. Carissa Blair discovers the color of love.

CARISSA. This is why we can't talk about anything. This is why my work is suffering and why I've been in a low grade depression for the last six months.

EDDIE. So that explains it.

CARISSA. Explains what?

EDDIE. This blue fixation you suddenly have.

CARISSA. What?

EDDIE. You're depression.

CARISSA. You think I have a fixation with blue because I'm depressed?

EDDIE. Yeah.

CARISSA. God, just admit you think love's red.

EDDIE. All through history people have associated sadness with the color blue.

CARISSA. You have absolutely no imagination.

EDDIE. I think if you're blue then love will look blue to you.

CARISSA. (*Laughing*) I can't believe we're having this conversation.

EDDIE. Passion might be red.

CARISSA. No, that's blue, too.

EDDIE. All through history—

CARISSA. Fuck history! This is my vision and my perspective.

Beat.

EDDIE. We can't do this anymore.

CARISSA. For God's sake—

EDDIE. What do I know about blue or perspective or your sacred
vision?

CARISSA. You never cared.

EDDIE. I did care. You pushed me out.

CARISSA. You made it a competition.

EDDIE. It got in the way.

CARISSA. What is it that you want from me? I'm just—I'm just
trying to do what I have to do—you know, I can't—

EDDIE. I don't know what I want anymore. Sometimes I think you're
too far gone, too far into it.

CARISSA. I haven't changed. This is what I've done, who I've been for
as long as you've known me.

EDDIE. No—I remember when you used to—you'd be driving and
you'd stop the car and get out if it started to rain just so you
could stand in it and feel it. And your mascara would start
dripping down your face and your hair'd get all scraggly and—
God! You used to—on Sunday afternoons when we'd be lying
around, you'd climb on top of me and we'd have this wild—
because you used to say that Sunday afternoons were only
good for making love. And you—you used to—

CARISSA. Just stop—

EDDIE. You used to put little notes in my jackets and I'd find them,
you know—sometimes weeks later. And you'd say things
like—like—

CARISSA & EDDIE. I love you.

EDDIE. Like I love you.

CARISSA. Something happened. I don't know.

EDDIE. I can't figure out what you became so afraid of.

CARISSA. Afraid?

EDDIE. You're afraid love just might be red.

CARISSA. Hot passionate red?

EDDIE. I need to feel it again.

CARISSA. It doesn't last. It always cools down to blue.

EDDIE. It's not that you can't get it back. It's that you don't want it.

CARISSA. I haven't changed!

EDDIE. Just cooled down?

CARISSA. Something like that.

EDDIE. It's not enough. I've been telling myself—it's just a phase—
        she'll come back. It'll get hot again. But it's been too long.
        You don't have it in you anymore. And what this is—I can't—
        I'm sorry.

Eddie begins to walk out.

CARISSA. Eddie, wait.

EDDIE. I love you. But I can't handle—you—you're in your own—
        there's no room for me.

CARISSA. So—what? This is it?

Beat.

EDDIE. I don't—Carissa, what is the point?

CARISSA. How 'bout the past three years. I mean I was working and I
        got caught up for awhile. I'm—I'm—I really shouldn't have to
        apologize for what I do. I don't walk into your classroom and
        demand your undivided attention when you're in the middle of
        your lecture.

EDDIE. But if you ever did, I'd drop everything for you.

CARISSA. If I ever did, it would be an emergency!

EDDIE. Don't pretend you want to keep this together.

CARISSA. I'm not.

EDDIE. You want this to end, too. You just wanted to be the one to say it.

CARISSA. No! You know how I feel. You know, I don't know what
  I'd do if we—if you—

EDDIE. I don't know either. I don't know anything anymore.

Carissa reaches for him. She tries to kiss him.

CARISSA. Let me, Eddie. Please.

EDDIE. You can't make it all go away by kissing and touching and
  fucking!

CARISSA. Don't leave me.

EDDIE. You left! You!

CARISSA. No. I'm here. I'm here now. I'll be all here for you. Please.

Carissa moves toward Eddie. Eddie backs away from her.

Please don't do this.

EDDIE. (*Mocking*) Am I hurting you? Are you feeling this?

Eddie moves closer to Carissa. She moves in. Eddie steps away.

CARISSA. God, please don't.

EDDIE. It hurts. I know.

*Eddie gets even closer but doesn't touch her. He leans to kiss her
but then decides not to.*

I know how it hurts.

CARISSA. Fuck you.

EDDIE. It was so simple. I just wanted to love you.

CARISSA. I wanted that, too. I want that now.

EDDIE. But I don't trust you anymore. Tonight—now maybe you
    want it, me. Tomorrow you'll be back here until three or four
    in the morning and I'll be in bed alone, staring at the ceiling
    wondering why I can't see what you see or feel what you feel
    when you're here alone in love with your work and yourself—
CARISSA. Why don't you just come right out and tell me you want
    me to make a choice.
EDDIE. Because I know what that choice would be. And I'd rather
    make it myself.
CARISSA. You're the one who's destroying this relationship. I
    shouldn't have to make a choice or even fucking compromise.
    You should understand.
EDDIE. I have tried to understand. I've tried to support you and to
    take care of all those practical details that you just didn't have
    the time or energy to take care of on your own.
CARISSA. Don't make it sound like you fucking have to dress me.
EDDIE. I tried to reach you way the fuck up there—where you live.
    Out there on your moon rising in fucking Aries. But you know
    what? I can't get there! All I know is that it still feels like shit
    when I'm lying in bed alone and remembering what those
    Sunday afternoons—what I felt—what you felt like.
CARISSA. Eddie—
EDDIE. Walking back here from the theatre, it just—I mean it was
    raining and I'm soaked because I thought—Carissa hates
    umbrellas and she should be here any second, any minute, any
    fucking hour now Carissa should be here! So I'm wet, the
    tickets are wet—and all I keep thinking is—is what the hell
    am I doing this for?
CARISSA. I forgot. I just forgot.
EDDIE. It dawned on me that there was no good reason to be standing
    on the curb—in the rain—waiting for you. I'm tired of waiting
    for you.
CARISSA. If this is about getting married—
EDDIE. You're not listening to me—

CARISSA. Because maybe it would be the right time to get married. I mean I haven't been ready, you know, and maybe now—maybe I could do it now.

EDDIE. That's fear. That's not love.

CARISSA. (*Going back to her canvas*) Fear... fear is green, I think.

EDDIE. Carissa—

CARISSA. It's not black. People think fear is black but it's green. It's all mixed up. Jealousy—so many people want jealousy to be green, but jealousy is—it's almost always—ninety percent of the time it's purple—like when red bleeds into blue.

EDDIE. I loved you so much.

CARISSA. What color do you think fear is?

EDDIE. Maybe it's red.

CARISSA. If you want it to be red then it'll be red.

EDDIE. I have to go.

CARISSA. Don't go.

EDDIE. I've made up my mind.

CARISSA. Unmake it.

EDDIE. Not this time.

CARISSA. You're my only touchstone. I won't be okay if—if you—

EDDIE. That's why you have Dr. Nod.

CARISSA. He moved—he moved six months ago. You never asked so I never said anything.

A couple beats.

I'm sorry. Is that what you want me to say? Is that the right answer? I'm sorry.

EDDIE. Yeah. You know. I think it's too late for sorry.

CARISSA. I don't want this.

Eddie leaves. The door slams behind him. Carissa stares at the canvas.

I was making this blue heart for you.

Black out.

ACT ONE - SCENE TWO
"SARAH & NOLAN"

The dining room of Nolan and Sarah's home.

The only thing on stage is a very large, elongated table, lavishly set for two, with candles (unlit), good china, crystal, and an empty vase in the center of the table. A window is in the backdrop. Upbeat music is heard from a music player.

At open, Sarah, 30s-40s, enters the dining room carrying a brown paper bag. She sets the bag down and rearranges some things on the table. She's laughing and singing to herself with the music. She's in a good mood. She goes to the window and looks out. Seeing someone, she waves.

She grabs the bag and pulls out a bundle of fake flowers. She stuffs them into the vase. She picks up a spoon and starts dancing around the table, singing into the spoon.

Nolan enters with a briefcase. She continues to sing. Nolan is confused yet also amused. He starts singing with her until they both end up laughing at themselves.

SARAH. Hi, honey.

NOLAN. What's wrong?

SARAH. Nothing at all. Just fooling around. I wonder if we still have this CD. I thought I'd lost it.

NOLAN. I think I downloaded it and threw out the disc. Does it matter?

SARAH. It does kind of—I mean, if it was mine. I never thought to put my name on my music or my books when we got married, but maybe I should have. It's just, at the time, doing that seemed dangerously close to a pre-nup and you were so opposed to that.

NOLAN. You're an attorney, Sarah. If it ever comes to that, I'm sure you'll have no problem getting what you want.

SARAH. I usually do get what I want.

NOLAN. That you do.

SARAH. How was work?

NOLAN. Work. It was just work.

SARAH. I have a surprise for you.

NOLAN. I can see that. You cooked.

SARAH. I'm tired of eating out. I thought tonight we could just relax and enjoy each other.

NOLAN. Great—that sounds wonderful.

SARAH. (Seductively) I'm even using our wedding china.

NOLAN. Have we ever used it?

SARAH. Never.

NOLAN. We should take it back.

SARAH. It really depends on the return policy. Usually stores won't take something back six years later.

NOLAN. Then let's use it.

SARAH. Stores are so unlike people that way. People will take things back five, six, even seven years later—but stores have that damn six month—or, God, at some stores you have to return things in thirty days. Like that's enough time to know if you want to keep something. Did you have a nice day?

NOLAN. It was just another day.

SARAH. Why don't you sit down and get comfortable.

Nolan goes to the table and sits.

NOLAN. Looks beautiful. What are you making?

Sarah sits across from him, at the other end of the table.

SARAH. I said it was a surprise.
NOLAN. I can't smell anything.
SARAH. That's because that oven in there seals off real tight when you close it. I read the directions.
NOLAN. It has directions?
SARAH. Yes, I never knew. Maybe I would've cooked something.
NOLAN. You hate cooking.
SARAH. I do. But I really need a change, and this is what I came up with.
NOLAN. It's a great idea.
SARAH. Nolan, tell me about Rhea.
NOLAN. What?
SARAH. Rhea. I'm so curious about her.
NOLAN. Let's not ruin a nice evening. You don't want to know about her.
SARAH. You never talk about her and I don't think it's healthy. I don't know anything about that time of your life.
NOLAN. I've forgotten it. I've forgotten her.

Sarah gets up and stands behind Nolan's chair.

SARAH. Take your jacket off. You look stiff.
NOLAN. Thank you.
SARAH. You probably haven't forgotten everything.
NOLAN. I think I have. Can we eat?

Sarah begins to rub Nolan's neck.

SARAH. She was beautiful.
NOLAN. She was young.

SARAH. How young would that be?

NOLAN. When I met her? Twenty-two.

SARAH. And when you married her?

NOLAN. Twenty-two and a half.

SARAH. Ten years ago?

NOLAN. Ten very long years ago.

SARAH. What was the date?

NOLAN. Of what?

SARAH. The day you married her.

NOLAN. I don't know May something.

SARAH. What day?

NOLAN. The 23rd, I think.

SARAH. Today's the 23rd.

NOLAN. So what? Why are you doing this? It has no bearing on us.

SARAH. Because you're so sexy when you flare your nostrils like that.
Hungry?

NOLAN. Yes, I am.

SARAH. It's almost done.

Sarah sits again.

Was she a good cook?

NOLAN. Sarah.

SARAH. Was she a good cook, Nolan?

NOLAN. She was. But that's all she wanted. She made a very nice
home.

SARAH. Nicer than me?

NOLAN. I'm not going to talk about this with you.

SARAH. I have nothing else to talk about tonight, honey.

NOLAN. Then I guess we won't be talking.

SARAH. Do you miss her?

NOLAN. Not particularly.

SARAH. What does that mean?

NOLAN. I don't think about her. You're my wife now. You've been my wife for six years. You're who I think about.

SARAH. But there must be moments when you think of her. Not that you miss her particularly—not particularly, right?

NOLAN. I've had enough, Sarah.

SARAH. Not that you miss her, all of her, but there are probably moments when I do something and you compare it to the way she did something and then—just maybe—you get a little pang.

NOLAN. I don't get pangs.

SARAH. Interesting. I better check dinner.

Sarah goes offstage, into the kitchen. Nolan is irritated.

NOLAN. (*Calling offstage*) I don't get pangs! Marrying you took the pang right out of me.

Sarah enters with an empty bowl and a large serving spoon.

SARAH. (*Entering*) You must have had a favorite dish that she made especially for you.

NOLAN. Can we eat, please?

SARAH. Beef stroganoff? Stir fry? Something with rice.

NOLAN. She made a damn good stir fry.

SARAH. No kidding?

NOLAN. What are we having?

SARAH. We're having pretend food.

Sarah starts scooping imaginary rice out of the empty bowl. She pretends to put it on Nolan's plate.

NOLAN. What is this?

SARAH. Hold on. I forgot the wine.

> *Sarah exits offstage and reenters with an empty bottle of wine.*
> *She pours nothing into Nolan's wine glass.*

NOLAN. Is this a joke?

SARAH. It is. It's a joke. A big huge joke, Nolan. See, I was going to make rice for dinner. I always thought carbs got a bad rap. But I couldn't actually make rice for dinner because Rhea stopped by this afternoon to pick up the rice steamer. Apparently it was hers and she just remembered that she had forgotten to get that from you seven long years ago.

NOLAN. Oh my God.

SARAH. So Rhea and I had a nice little chat.

NOLAN. Oh my God.

SARAH. She's a very nice person. I'm surprised you left her. But oh! That's right, she clarified that it was she who left you. In fact, she only left the rice steamer because she thought it would make you realize what you would be missing without her. Poor thing. It all came down to rice for her.

NOLAN. Oh my God.

SARAH. You keep saying that. I hate redundancy.

NOLAN. She was—she was here?

SARAH. I'm a lawyer. I have no imagination. I wouldn't make it up.

NOLAN. I just think it's strange.

SARAH. Don't be silly. It was—enlightening—really.

NOLAN. Great. Let's eat.

SARAH. She's done very well for herself. She owns her own travel agency. And she has twenty employees who do all the work for her and she just—just travels and goes places. Like here.

NOLAN. Really—I thought she would've remarried by now.

SARAH. No. It took her a long time to—what was it—to get into the deepest caverns of her psyche.

NOLAN. Caverns? She said caverns?

SARAH. It's been a difficult recovery, but I guess she has someone in her life now. And it's a woman.

NOLAN. What?

SARAH. She's exploring.

NOLAN. Uhuh.

SARAH. She's actually a very candid bisexual.

NOLAN. I did—wow—I did wonder about her.

SARAH. I bet you did.

Nolan gets up and puts on his jacket.

NOLAN. There, honey. Now you see. I was never meant to be with her. She's always been a little off. Where should we eat?

SARAH. I'm not hungry.

NOLAN. Well, I'm starving.

SARAH. But look how pretty my table looks.

NOLAN. It's very pretty. Let's go.

SARAH. Let's just sit here and look at it.

NOLAN. There's no food. It's pretty but it's empty.

SARAH. Exactly.

NOLAN. What? What, Sarah? Are you trying to make a point here?

SARAH. Let's see. Pretty but empty.

NOLAN. Is this some comment on Rhea because I think the statute of limitations on insulting your spouse's ex is somewhere around two years.

SARAH. I'm not talking about Rhea, honey. I'm talking about us.

NOLAN. That's us, is it? Pretty but empty?

SARAH. Don't you think?

NOLAN. No. I don't think. I think we make a damn good couple. I think we understand each other. I think we have a lot in common. I think we can have in depth discussions about things that are much, much—more—

SARAH. In depth?

NOLAN. Much more in depth than stir fry!

SARAH. I happen to like stir fry.

NOLAN. I need to go back on anti-depressants.

SARAH. Where would you like to eat?

NOLAN. Mackie's.

SARAH. I saw a cockroach there. I want fast food. Very, very fast food.

NOLAN. I don't care anymore. Can we just go?

SARAH. Let me turn off the oven.

NOLAN. Just forget it! Just fucking forget it!

SARAH. Alright, Nolan.

Beat.

She recognized my ring.

NOLAN. Of course she did.

SARAH. Because it was her ring.

NOLAN. So.

SARAH. You gave me her ring!

NOLAN. I bought that ring as a gift—to my wife. When she wasn't my wife anymore, I took it back. When you became my wife, I gave it to you.

SARAH. You don't even think there's anything wrong with that.

NOLAN. No.

SARAH. You gave it to her as a gift.

NOLAN. No. I gave it to her as a symbol.

SARAH. That's what I thought you'd say. Sit down. I have something for you.

NOLAN. I don't want to sit down.

SARAH. Then stand there.

Sarah exits offstage. Nolan hurls a chair across the room. Sarah reenters with a brand new suitcase. The price tag dangles from the handle.

SARAH. Really, Nolan. Those are my antique chairs.

NOLAN. Our antique chairs.

SARAH. I'll figure that out later.

NOLAN. Figure what out?

SARAH. Don't be rude. I'm giving you a present.

NOLAN. A suitcase?

SARAH. It's not just any suitcase. It's the one we saw at the mall last weekend and you went on and on about how you needed good luggage and how much you liked this.

NOLAN. It's very nice. Thank you.

SARAH. Oh stop. It's no big deal. I mean it's empty, come on.

NOLAN. But it's too much.

SARAH. No, it's not. It's really not.

Nolan hugs Sarah awkwardly.

NOLAN. I'm sorry Rhea caught you off guard.

SARAH. It's okay. It turns out we have all kinds of things in common.

NOLAN. What does that mean?

SARAH. Well, I mean, when we started comparing notes.

NOLAN. Oh my God.

SARAH. Let's see—dirty underwear kicked under the bed. Disgusting slurping noise when you eat cereal. Neanderthal way you throw things when you get pissed. God, we bonded.

NOLAN. I don't like where you're going with this.

SARAH. As we talked—I began to think stupid little Rhea was actually the smart one.

NOLAN. What is your point? Get to the point!

SARAH. Do you like your suitcase?

NOLAN. It's great.

SARAH. Use it.

NOLAN. Pardon me.

SARAH. Why don't you go see what you can fill it up with. You can
start with the dirty underwear under the bed.
NOLAN. You want me to—

Sarah nods. She takes off her wedding ring and hands it to him.

SARAH. Pass it on.
NOLAN. What are you doing?
SARAH. This suitcase is a gift and a symbol. Get it?
NOLAN. No.
SARAH. Nolan—I'm leaving you.
NOLAN. You want to get a divorce? You don't love me?
SARAH. Yes. I don't.
NOLAN. Even though I love you.
SARAH. Basically—yes.
NOLAN. Forever? I mean we could separate for awhile and see how it
goes.
SARAH. That would just prolong the inevitable.
NOLAN. You'll miss me.
SARAH. Maybe. Maybe not.
NOLAN. I'll change.
SARAH. Nolan, you swallow people whole and then you throw them
up. I don't want that to happen to me and I can feel it coming.
I'm lodged in right next to your esophagus and any second
now—
NOLAN. That is such a bad metaphor. You are so bad at that.
SARAH. But I'm really good at goodbye. Goodbye.

*Sarah grabs her purse from under the table, looks at the suitcase,
and then grabs that too.*

NOLAN. That's my suitcase.
SARAH. It was. I just realized it matches my new shoes.
NOLAN. You're taking my suitcase back?

SARAH. Better now than in five years. Besides I need it for my trip.

NOLAN. What trip?

SARAH. My trip to the Bahamas. Rhea got me a great deal.

NOLAN. This can't be happening.

SARAH. I'm sure reality will sink in once you're served. Now I have
to run, honey. I have a plane to catch.

Sarah begins to leave. Her back is to Nolan.

NOLAN. God damn it!

*Nolan picks up a piece of the china—a plate—and goes to throw
it on the ground. Sarah senses this though her back is to him. She
stops, her back still to him.*

SARAH. You can't take it back if it's broken.

Sarah exits. Black out.

ACT ONE - SCENE THREE
"WYNNE & FELIX"

> *The study/office of Felix's Upper West Side apartment. Four a.m.*
>
> *At open, Felix sits in his oversized desk chair at his very large desk. A book lies open across his chest. His head is tipped back. He sleeps.*
>
> *A laptop computer is on the desk, along with books, papers, files. All in clutters and stacks. It is the only thing on a dim stage.*
>
> *Soft classical music comes from the small portable stereo crammed precariously on the desktop.*
>
> *Wynne, 20ish, enters in a white nightgown. She is a wisp, nymph-like and almost unreal.*
>
> *She goes to Felix and quietly rummages through his papers, looking for something but not finding it. Felix stirs and she quickly reaches to turn off the music, as if that was what she meant to do. Felix wakes up.*

FELIX. What are you doing? What time is it?
WYNNE. It's four.
FELIX. What time is it?
WYNNE. It's four in the morning.
FELIX. I fell asleep.
WYNNE. I was thinking of going for a walk. Come with me.

FELIX. Right now?

WYNNE. You don't want to come with me?

> *Felix reaches for her.*

FELIX. Wynne, sweetie, let's go to bed—

WYNNE. No.

FELIX. Then we'll talk. I'm awake now. What is it?

WYNNE. I don't wanna talk. You can go to bed. I'll stay here.

> *Wynne sinks to the floor and sits with her legs crossed. She closes
> her eyes.*

FELIX. What are you doing?

WYNNE. Breathing.

FELIX. Okay. You breathe. I'm going to bed. Good night.

WYNNE. It's good morning.

FELIX. Good morning.

WYNNE. It's not really. It's not good.

FELIX. I don't know yet.

WYNNE. Can't you just feel what a day's gonna be like? I always can.
  Especially now, around this time—just until dawn.

FELIX. I find this time of night oppressive.

> *She stands again. Stretches.*

WYNNE. Not me. This is when I like to come out.

FELIX. Come out?

WYNNE. (*Laughs*) I usually get up around now.

FELIX. You do—you get up at four? Why in the world—

WYNNE. I don't know why-in-the-world I do it. I just do it, because
  I feel better. Then I go back to bed before the sun—

FELIX. Maybe you're sleepwalking.

WYNNE. (*smiles*) I sleepwalk when I'm awake.

FELIX. All the time you've been staying with me you've been up at
this hour?

WYNNE. Yes. So?

FELIX. You should've told me.

WYNNE. I have lots of secrets.

Wynne laughs.

Just now I thought about cutting your hair off. Like Delilah.

FELIX. You would never do that, would you?

WYNNE. If the spirit moved me.

FELIX. Do you come in here when you're up wandering around?

WYNNE. I said I have lots of secrets.

FELIX. Answer the question.

WYNNE. We all have lots of secrets, don't we?

FELIX. This isn't funny. Are you okay? Are we okay here?

WYNNE. Whatever could you mean?

Felix grabs her and looks at the inside of her arms.

FELIX. You need to tell me—

WYNNE. Is this how you put me in my place? Wanna check between
my toes, too?

FELIX. Just tell me if you—

WYNNE. I haven't touched it. Even when I feel like I'll die, I don't
touch it. And it's not like I can't get it.

*Felix holds on to her. She's limp, like she could slip through his
arms and float away.*

FELIX. Don't scare me.

WYNNE. (*Pulling away*) Sometimes I think it's too late. I don't know if it's a body I need or if it's a soul.

FELIX. You don't need anything. You're perfect.

WYNNE. What were you working on? Your novel or your column?

FELIX. My novel.

WYNNE. When are you going to finish your novel?

FELIX. I'm waiting for it to finish itself. Soon.

WYNNE. How will it end? Do you know?

FELIX. I'm not sure yet.

WYNNE. Is it a sad ending?

FELIX. Bittersweet. Most likely.

WYNNE. I think so, too.

Beat. Felix studies Wynne, unsure of her.

FELIX. What do you do when you get up—when you get up at four?

WYNNE. Wander mostly.

FELIX. Inside?

WYNNE. Or outside.

FELIX. I'm asking you again. Do you come in here?

WYNNE. The parlor of the king? There's nothing interesting here.

FELIX. Then why'd you come in here tonight?

WYNNE. For you. I came for you.

Felix strokes her face softly.

FELIX. I don't believe you—but God, I love you.

WYNNE. I don't want you to say that anymore.

FELIX. Why?

WYNNE. I don't like it.

FELIX. I need to say it.

WYNNE. I need you to stop saying it. I feel your—your attachment.

Reaching for her. She moves away.

FELIX. Let me touch you.

WYNNE. Stop it, Felix. I said no.

FELIX. I am trying so hard to understand you.

WYNNE. I don't want understanding. I want something—something beyond all your words and labels.

FELIX. We have that. I think we have that.

WYNNE. You're a writer. You can never have it. You have to name everything so you can feel better about yourself. Your whole life is about capturing and containing.

FELIX. You're wrong. I know what can never be captured. I know that thing better than anyone because I'm always scribbling around it.

WYNNE. I'm tired of words. Tired of your scribbling.

FELIX. I'm sorry to hear you say that.

WYNNE. I wake up at four in the morning so I can feel something. It's something—it's God, I think.

FELIX. God?

WYNNE. It's God and it's nothing. Everything's so perfectly still.

FELIX. I wish I could give you what you're looking for—what you want.

WYNNE. I want to be free.

FELIX. Free—as in—not in this relationship?

WYNNE. There you go again, ruining it with words.

FELIX. We're having a conversation, aren't we? As far as I know, the way you do that is by communicating. Dialoguing. You say something, I respond. Or vice versa. We have ideas and we put words to them and we express what's on our minds.

WYNNE. You build walls with your words.

FELIX. Paper walls, Wynne. You exhale and they blow away.

WYNNE. You kill me with your words.

FELIX. Don't say that.

Beat.

WYNNE. I can't stay here.

FELIX. I knew this was coming.

WYNNE. I get restless.

FELIX. I know.

WYNNE. And when all those words start closing in on me, I think I could do something—something that would be very bad.

FELIX. Like what? Cheat on me? Kill yourself? What does that mean?

WYNNE. I can't let you talk me into love. Not your kind of love anyway.

FELIX. I could love you—that's what you said... God! I wish you had never said that to me.

WYNNE. It was a mistake. That first night.

FELIX. I thought it was because I left you a fifty dollar tip.

WYNNE. You left me fifty because you stiffed me the night before.

FELIX. My food was ice cold.

WYNNE. That wasn't my fault.

FELIX. I realized that when you came running after me. You were out of breath, saying you needed to rest.

WYNNE. I did—I needed to rest.

FELIX. I knew then. I knew what kind of woman you were.

WYNNE. I'm not a kind.

FELIX. That's right. You move when the spirit calls. To or from. Forward or backward. Unpredictably like the wind.

WYNNE. I stayed with you the longest. I might come back.

FELIX. You might?

WYNNE. I don't give explanations.

FELIX. No, what you give is false hope. That's what you gave me— although it felt a lot like real hope until this morning.

WYNNE. I can't explain what happened between us.

FELIX. I don't need an explanation. God, I don't need more words either. I want to touch you. Like we touched in the beginning.

WYNNE. I remember.

FELIX. This—I wasn't ready for this.

WYNNE. What you wrote on page fourteen... That's not true.

Beat.

FELIX. I wanted to surprise you.

WYNNE. You did.

FELIX. You weren't supposed to see it. It's not done.

Beat.

WYNNE. At first I was flattered that the book was about me. But that's not me.

FELIX. I was trying to figure you out and it's the only way I knew how to do it.

WYNNE. I would rather be in your imagination—not—not on those pages, see, 'cause those words—they crush me. They're too binding. And mostly they're wrong. Even if they were right, they'd be wrong.

FELIX. They're right to me.

WYNNE. I knew this would happen.

FELIX. You make a commitment to someone—

WYNNE. I don't make commitments. I never have.

FELIX. What? You're completely dictated by your nerve endings?

WYNNE. Yes, I am.

FELIX. No wonder you were a fucking junkie for so long.

Beat.

WYNNE. Words, words... words.

FELIX. Yeah, well those words mean something. They say something about your character.

WYNNE. No, they don't. They say something about your perception of me.

FELIX. Oh—okay. I'm beginning to see how this works. This is how you avoid taking responsibility for yourself. You just don't name it. You don't call it what it is!

WYNNE. I let life happen. I let things be. And I try—I try very hard to trust my instincts and to just go with—

Felix grabs her in frustration.

FELIX. With what? The flow?

WYNNE. That's a cliché. It's a cliché because people are too unoriginal to come up with another way of saying what they shouldn't even bother trying to say in the first place.

FELIX. What about love?

WYNNE. God, nothing, and love. It's the same.

FELIX. No, it's not.

WYNNE. Let me go.

Beat. Felix releases her and steps back.

FELIX. I love you. I don't God you or nothing you. I love you. See you lose something in the transfer. It's not the same.

WYNNE. If you lose something in the transfer then it's not love. It's desire or possession or—

FELIX. That's all part of love.

WYNNE. Not pure love.

FELIX. There's no such thing as pure love.

WYNNE. It's nothing and everything.

FELIX. Keep going. Negate me out of your life. You have a system— you'd never admit it, but you have the perfect system for deconstructing everything that's worth anything. You know, Wynne, for a long time this little game, this little dance we've been doing has been comfortable and safe even—but it's never been real, has it? And I need the realness of life. It energizes me and it helps me remember that I'm alive. And it's fucking—

it's the best fucking feeling in the world to sit down and to articulate, to try to make sense of the real things. Of that desk and this paper and you and the way you smell after you get out of the shower and you're lying in bed next to me. Those are the things that matter to me. Not bizarre impressions from another dimension. I don't care about that. I care about—just finding my way through life. That's hard enough. And you—it's like I lost my grounding. At first, I loved that you did that to me. God, it was so fucking magical and—ecstasy. You were my ecstasy. And maybe I was wrong for trying so hard to find a name for you, for labeling you, for putting you in the god damn book—but I couldn't help it. You kept floating away from me and I kept trying to pull you back, and I did it by writing—writing you.

WYNNE. The book is good. It's a good lie. People will love it and you're whole life will change. You won't want me back then.

FELIX. Don't twist this around.

WYNNE. I'm not saying this has to be forever. I never said that.

FELIX. But if this is it—if this is it, it has to be something a hell of a lot more concrete than that.

WYNNE. You don't want me to come back?

FELIX. No. Not if we end this now. I don't ever want you to come back. I'm not another fix.

WYNNE. Don't make comparisons like that. It's not fair.

FELIX. I just need to know that this isn't about wanting to go back out there and—

WYNNE. I said I'm done with it.

FELIX. But those are just words after all.

WYNNE. Then I guess it's hard to say.

Beat.

FELIX. Where will you go?

WYNNE. Somewhere far away.

FELIX. Why don't you go now.

WYNNE. I'm not ready to go now.

FELIX. The spirit isn't moving you?

WYNNE. No.

FELIX. Well, maybe I can speed the process up.

> *Felix grabs Wynne's arm and begins to pull her out of the room.*

WYNNE. You're hurting me. Don't!

> *Felix lets go.*

FELIX. I'm sorry.

> *Wynne takes a swing at Felix. Felix grabs her and kisses her.*
> *They begin to kiss but Wynne pulls away suddenly.*

WYNNE. I can't.

FELIX. Yeah—for a minute—I thought—

WYNNE. I'm sorry.

FELIX. I can't win, can I?

WYNNE. This is the only way I know to save myself.

FELIX. By killing me.

> *Beat.*

I'm going to bed. Good night.

> *Felix walks toward the bedroom.*

WYNNE. Good morning.

Felix stops and turns toward her.

FELIX. Goodbye.

Black out. End of Act One.

Act Two

about a year later

ACT TWO - SCENE ONE
"FELIX & SARAH"

Felix's study/office. One year later.

Just like before. The same very large desk is on stage, still cluttered with books and paper, along with a laptop computer, a desk lamp (the light is on), and an alarm clock. In addition, a bottle of cognac sits on the desk.

Beethoven's "Fur Elise" plays. Felix and Sarah enter together. Felix is holding Sarah's suitcase, the one she was going to give Nolan in Act One. Sarah looks around.

SARAH. And this is your office?

FELIX. Or, as it was once referred to, the parlor of the king. Can I interest you in some cognac?

SARAH. (*Checks her cell phone*) Oh—it's later than I expected. I should only stay for a few minutes. My plane leaves in a couple hours and you never know how long that security line will be.

FELIX. One drink?

SARAH. I better not.

FELIX. Just a quick one.

SARAH. I really can't—but thank you for the offer and for the tour, your highness.

FELIX. Old friends, easy access.

SARAH. I feel special.

FELIX. You are special.

SARAH. Well, thank you.

FELIX. Wanna dance?

Felix awkwardly puts down Sarah's suitcase.

SARAH. Have you been holding my suitcase this whole time?

FELIX. I have.

SARAH. I meant to leave it in the car.

FELIX. I didn't want it to get stolen.

SARAH. Stolen? In this neighborhood?

FELIX. This is beautiful luggage.

SARAH. Thank you. I like it.

FELIX. It goes nicely with your shoes.

SARAH. Well—yes. So it does.

FELIX. Where were we?

SARAH. You asked me to dance, but I can't. I really do have a plane
        to catch.

FELIX. One dance.

SARAH. (*Laughing*) Do you always leave the music on?

FELIX. I do. It's good feng shui.

SARAH. Is that true?

FELIX. I have no idea.

Felix turns off the music.

SARAH. You must spend a lot of time in here—writing?

FELIX. Writing? God, no. Just drinking.

SARAH. Sounds lonely.

FELIX. It is—which inspires me to write so I don't have to think
        about being lonely.

SARAH. You turned out to be a great writer. Who knew?

FELIX. I'm just another writer.

SARAH. *No Way to Win* is not just another book.

FELIX. Give it time.

SARAH. No, no. This one will stay on the best-seller list for years.

FELIX. I have to admit it's a little disconcerting to think of people
        from my past reading my books.

SARAH. I must have told every single person in that bookstore that you were my first lo—that you were an old friend from college.

Felix takes the bottle of cognac and opens it.

FELIX. The best thing about that story is that actual people were looking at books in a bookstore.

SARAH. Well, I don't think those two or three *actual* people believed me. You know, maybe I will have some cognac.

Felix grabs the bottle of cognac and hands it to Sarah.

SARAH. Do you have a glass?

FELIX. In the kitchen. Just take a swig.

SARAH. Drinking cognac from the bottle is disgusting.

FELIX. Geez, so picky. It didn't bother you in college.

SARAH. Did we drink cognac in college?

FELIX. We drank rubbing alcohol in college—whatever it took. The cheaper the better.

SARAH. This doesn't look cheap.

FELIX. It was a very expensive gift. We should drink it.

Felix drinks.

SARAH. Okay. But for the record, I did not drink rubbing alcohol.

Sarah drinks.

FELIX. Thank you for having dinner with me.

SARAH. Thank you for not saying anything when I sent my food back.

FELIX. It was charming.

SARAH. It was ice cold.

FELIX. It's amazing how I feel completely relaxed with you—after all these years.

SARAH. I'm sure I'll feel completely relaxed after this cognac.

Sarah downs more of the cognac.

FELIX. I'm glad you e-mailed.

SARAH. I'm glad you e-mailed back.

FELIX. A number of times.

SARAH. It was odd to finally talk on the phone.

FELIX. I'm glad you took my call.

SARAH. Well, I knew I'd have a little time in New York and what the hell, right?

FELIX. What the hell.

SARAH. Felix.

FELIX. Hmm.

SARAH. I know you probably had all kinds of people coming out of the woodwork once you hit the best-seller list.

FELIX. I hadn't noticed.

SARAH. With that picture on the insert—

FELIX. They touched it up—

SARAH. And all the hype—

FELIX. It's all hype—

SARAH. I contacted you because it's such a good book.

FELIX. I would've looked you up eventually. I'm sure I would've.

SARAH. Maybe.

FELIX. I would have. Just to find out if you became everything you said you would. And you have.

SARAH. Professionally, you mean.

FELIX. You always had a one track mind.

SARAH. I was never good with that balancing act. Never too good with whatever that takes. Some parts of my life played out better than other parts. That's all.

FELIX. Common ground. I'll drink to that.

Felix drinks more cognac.

SARAH. I better not have anymore.

Gesturing.

Pretend cheers.

FELIX. We don't have to pretend with each other, do we?
SARAH. What?
FELIX. I don't know. We've been going back and forth all night. We
    were always good at that.
SARAH. At what?
FELIX. At words. Now that we're a little smarter and a lot older,
    we're even better, I think. Maybe it is pretend. Pretend
    banter. Pretend business talk. It's all filler.
SARAH. Filler?
FELIX. Filler—so that I don't have to acknowledge that I was
    mortified when you sent your food back.
SARAH. Or that I was terrified to see you.
FELIX. Terrified?
SARAH. You were mortified when I sent my food back?
FELIX. A little.
SARAH. I think I will have another drink.
FELIX. Good. Take another flight.
SARAH. No, I'll drink it fast and fly drunk. Why not?
FELIX. Maybe you need a vacation.
SARAH. You and me both.
FELIX. Exactly. You and I should go on vacation.
SARAH. Stop it.
FELIX. When was your last one?

SARAH. Oh, the Bahamas, I guess.

FELIX. With your ex-husband?

SARAH. No, my ex-wife—I mean his ex-wife. Not really with her. She got me the package—I mean the deal. It's a very long story. He gave me her ring.

FELIX. Who?

SARAH. My ex-husband Nolan. He gave me his ex-wife's ring.

FELIX. Economical.

SARAH. Very cheap.

FELIX. I can't believe you let him give you a ring you didn't choose.

SARAH. It was in the early days, when I trusted his judgment and the sex was still good.

FELIX. How did you find out?

SARAH. *(smiles)* About the sex?

FELIX. About the ring.

SARAH. Because of the rice.

FELIX. Wait—what are we talking about?

SARAH. I didn't even know we had a rice steamer let alone hers. Anyway, she saw my ring and told me it was her ring. I told Nolan and he was stupid enough to admit it and the rest is history.

FELIX. Nothing you've said makes any sense, and yet I could listen to you all night.

SARAH. And you are exactly the same.

FELIX. I don't know about that.

SARAH. You look the same.

FELIX. You look even better than I remember.

SARAH. Is that supposed to be seductive or insulting?

FELIX. I thought insults were seductive.

SARAH. Can't resist, can you? Words, words, words!

FELIX. I've heard that somewhere before.

SARAH. I know exactly what you're doing. This is a test.

FELIX. Of whether or not you still find me irresistible?

SARAH. You must mean egotistical.

FELIX. *(smiles)* I think you're upset.

SARAH. What? I am *not* upset.

FELIX. Don't let our painful parting prejudice you now.

SARAH. Was it painful? Please.

FELIX. Very nice alliteration.

SARAH. You like that? I can keep up with you.

FELIX. Do you recall our first time?

SARAH. Perhaps.

FELIX. Were you a virgin?

SARAH. Pardon?

FELIX. I was.

SARAH. That would explain your performance.

FELIX. Only three times prior.

SARAH. That makes you *almost* a virgin.

FELIX. We were young.

SARAH. Yes, look how much we've grown and learned.

FELIX. About love and whatnot.

SARAH. More about whatnot.

FELIX. I am dying to kiss you.

SARAH. Just do it already.

Felix leans into Sarah. Their lips meet gently.

FELIX. Were we in love?

SARAH. Were we?

FELIX. I was probably too afraid to admit it. I didn't have as many
      words in those days. Now I have a name for everything.

SARAH. For love?

FELIX. A bad name for love.

SARAH. Because your muse ran away?

FELIX. She was a figment of my imagination. Never could quite get a
      hold of her. The actual never lives up to the ideal anyway. Not
      exactly. The book is never what you intended it to be. The
      love is never what you fantasized. I don't know if naming it

destroys it, but it certainly changes it. Puts a limit on it. Creates a context for it. But it's all the same in the end—constant change. What people get wrong is not that they fear the love but the whatnot. The end of love. The whatnot end of love.

SARAH. Is that why you called the book *No Way to Win*?

FELIX. One of the reasons.

SARAH. So I shouldn't expect a sequel?

FELIX. A sequel—no. A feature film—maybe.

SARAH. Nothing is sacred.

FELIX. I think that's my problem.

Beat.

SARAH. I never thought I'd see you again. I figured you were just another should have been—another closed door—

FELIX. And here we are. I like the profound circularity of it.

SARAH. I don't give people second chances.

FELIX. Let's call it a first chance. A mid-life first chance.

SARAH. That would screw everything up— I decided many years ago that in some parallel universe we're married with a couple kids.

FELIX. Really?

SARAH. Happily even.

FELIX. And from someone as cynical as you?

SARAH. Idealism is my dark secret. Don't tell.

FELIX. I must have let you down.

SARAH. What?

FELIX. I just realized—I let you down.

SARAH. I recovered.

FELIX. I hurt you and I'm sorry.

Beat.

SARAH. No one has ever said that to me.

FELIX. I don't think I've ever said it to anyone.

SARAH. I didn't expect that but thank you.

> *Beat.*

Well. I should go—I should just go. Seeing you was so nice. A little flirting, a little drinking, a little revelation—just the perfect amount of revelation—and now back to reality.

> *Sarah raises the bottle of cognac—*

Real cheers.

> *Felix reaches for the bottle. They linger there for a moment until Sarah takes one last swig from the cognac bottle.*

FELIX. I'd love it if you would stay.

> *Beat.*

SARAH. Stay here?

FELIX. I'd love it.

SARAH. Is that a comment or an offer?

FELIX. I'll go with offer.

SARAH. Do you have ulterior motives?

FELIX. Definitely.

SARAH. That makes it very tempting.

FELIX. Than say yes.

SARAH. I have a dentist appointment.

FELIX. On Saturday?

SARAH. Alright, fine. The cleaning lady is coming and she doesn't have a key. I left a big mess—

FELIX. Leave it. Let things be messy.

SARAH. You mean us? We're messy. This is a big mess, isn't it? It is. Shit.

FELIX. Don't panic. Two days in New York and then you can get back to your messy house in L.A.

SARAH. I just realized something.

FELIX. Another revelation? You may be going over your allotted amount.

SARAH. I'm much better at leaving than at staying.

FELIX. See, already I've given you deep insight into yourself.

SARAH. Hmm. What deep insights do you have?

FELIX. Well, for one, the time wasn't right for us twenty—

SARAH. Twenty-five—

FELIX. Twenty something years ago. We were young and stupid. But now—who knows. We could walk away and then in five, ten years we'll bump into each other at an airport or in a restaurant or in some office building in the elevator.

SARAH. That's very fatalistic.

FELIX. Then how about if I said I think you are a beautiful woman—I always have—and maybe we won't talk to each other ever again. We could still have one hell of a weekend.

SARAH. That's the problem. I'm already hoping we will talk to each other again.

Beat. Felix doesn't know how to respond.

Okay, there it is. That will be the final revelation. I've said too much and now I'm leaving.

Sarah turns to go but Felix stops her.

FELIX. If you leave here tonight and get back on that plane, I'll be thinking about you. I'll be remembering how you picked the legs off the calamari and that your lipstick made a perfect imprint on your wine glass, and when I get back in my car, I'll still smell that incredible perfume you're wearing. I've never met a woman like you—I mean you have so much to say— granted it's usually caustic and biting, but I love that about you.

SARAH. I'm not the same person I was.

FELIX. No, you're not. You're even better, remember?

SARAH. I'm beginning to think you are, too.

FELIX. You would not believe how much better.

SARAH. You think so? We'll see—

Felix takes Sarah in his arms. Sarah holds Felix tightly.

FELIX. Wanna dance now?

SARAH. I do.

Black out.

ACT TWO - SCENE TWO
"NOLAN & CARISSA"

Nolan's dining room. One year later.

*On stage is the oversized dining table, just as Sarah left it—with wedding china, unlit candles, and fake flowers. A red jacket is thrown over one of the dining room chairs and a copy of Felix's book **No Way to Win** sits on the seat of the same chair.*

In the backdrop is the window.

At open, Nolan stands near the window and looks out to a gloomy Sunday afternoon. An old standard plays from the music player. He shakes his head at his own masochistic behavior and turns the music off.

Looking out the window, he notices something. He grabs his jacket off the chair and runs out of the house returning with Carissa. Nolan has thrown his red jacket over Carissa, shielding her from the rain outside.

Carissa is wet and barefoot.

NOLAN. Why are you laughing? No, really. What's so funny?

CARISSA. I don't know—I just—

NOLAN. What, come on.

CARISSA. You're really sweet.

NOLAN. You're laughing at me?

CARISSA. No, no. Well—yeah—no. I don't know.

NOLAN. You're really wet.

CARISSA. I feel silly. Here—

Carissa hands him his jacket.

What?

Beat. Nolan stares at Carissa.

NOLAN. Nothing. Sorry.
CARISSA. This is too funny.

Carissa notices the table.

You're expecting someone. I gotta go.

NOLAN. No. Why don't you use my phone?
CARISSA. Oh, okay. Why do I want to use your phone?
NOLAN. Don't you need to call someone for your car?
CARISSA. I have a phone.
NOLAN. Of course.
CARISSA. And there's nothing wrong with my car.
NOLAN. Your car—isn't your car broken?
CARISSA. (*Laughing*) No. Oh God, you thought my—no.
NOLAN. It's just stopped in the street there.
CARISSA. It's fine.
NOLAN. It's blocking a driveway, I think—
CARISSA. I just had the impulse to get out of my car. It's such a
        beautiful neighborhood. Such beautiful homes.
NOLAN. Wow. Okay, I feel like an idiot.
CARISSA. No, please. It was an easy mistake. I—
NOLAN. I'm sorry.
CARISSA. Don't be, really.
NOLAN. I saw you there—standing there and it's raining—
CARISSA. I like the rain.

NOLAN. It was gonna get dark.

CARISSA. Eventually, yeah.

NOLAN. Eventually—so I thought maybe you needed some help.

CARISSA. I should just go.

NOLAN. No!

Beat.

I mean. Stay—if you want.

CARISSA. (*Smiles*) What's your name?

NOLAN. Nolan.

CARISSA. I feel like we should be in a bar or something. So what's
    your sign?

NOLAN. Excuse me?

CARISSA. I'm a Sagittarius with my moon rising in Aries. Which
    basically means I'm burning my candle at both ends. I think
    that's why I love the rain. It cools me down.

NOLAN. I should've asked before I grabbed you.

CARISSA. No, no. It's okay. You're probably one of those rescuing
    signs.

NOLAN. No, I'm an accountant.

CARISSA. Oh.

NOLAN. I usually overlook people with broken down cars who are
    standing like that—in the middle of—

CARISSA. (*laughs*) You should. You don't know who you can trust.

NOLAN. Yeah.

CARISSA. My name's Carissa.

NOLAN. Carissa.

CARISSA. So why didn't you overlook me?

NOLAN. I don't know. You looked so wet and kind of dazed or lost,
    so I just—

CARISSA. I get that glaze in my eyes. I tune out.

NOLAN. But that's a good thing?

CARISSA. It works for me.

> *Carissa reaches into her tee shirt pocket and pulls out a pack of very soggy cigarettes.*

Shit. They're wet—I forgot—

NOLAN. I have some somewhere. Let's see—where did those go—Here.

> *Nolan pulls a pack of cigarettes out of his jacket and hands one to Carissa.*

CARISSA. That's good. You smoke.

NOLAN. I don't know how good it is.

CARISSA. I mean you're right. We shouldn't smoke.

NOLAN. I didn't use to. I did for awhile and then I quit when I got married.

CARISSA. Oh! You're married?

NOLAN. No, I started again—smoking—about six months ago when the divorce was final. Then I quit again last week. You can keep those.

CARISSA. Thank you.

NOLAN. Yeah. You know, you think you know someone and then BAM—I mean it's like they've been wearing this body and suddenly the real person comes out.

CARISSA. People change.

NOLAN. I guess. Yeah.

CARISSA. Do you miss her?

NOLAN. No. Not particu—not really.

> *Carissa notices the finely set table again.*

CARISSA. I feel like I'm interrupting. You're probably cooking dinner
    for whoever you're expecting.
NOLAN. I'm not expecting anyone.
CARISSA. But I just thought—the table is set so beautifully.

Carissa moves toward the table.

What lovely silk flowers.

NOLAN. I wondered why those hadn't died.
CARISSA. These should last.
NOLAN. Not much like love.
CARISSA. Not much.
NOLAN. I left the table like that. It's a long story—I never really had
    the energy to undo it.
CARISSA. Well, it looks so nice.
NOLAN. I didn't think she'd come back. I take that back. I did think
    she'd come back but then after a couple months—you know—
CARISSA. How long has it been?
NOLAN. A year.
CARISSA. Where is she now?
NOLAN. From what I hear, she's spending some time in New York.
CARISSA. I got dumped awhile ago, too.
NOLAN. You did? That's great—I mean that's awful, but—I mean
    it's great because you understand.
CARISSA. Yeah.
NOLAN. Are you hungry? I could find something.
CARISSA. Sure.
NOLAN. I eat out a lot, but I think I have some cheese in the fridge.
CARISSA. Okay.
NOLAN. Cheese is good?
CARISSA. Sure.
NOLAN. Okay. That was easy.

CARISSA. I'm always easy on Sunday afternoons.

Beat.

NOLAN. Oh? I mean, you're right—it feels like an easy Sunday. Sort
of soggy and blue...
CARISSA. Sort of ice blue like—
NOLAN. Right—like—like ice.
CARISSA. Like the color of love.
NOLAN. Or sure—like that.

Beat.

Let me get the cheese.

*Nolan exits offstage. Carissa goes to the table and sits down,
inadvertently sitting on a copy of* **No Way to Win** *. She picks
up the book and starts thumbing through it.*

CARISSA. (*Calling offstage*) Need some help?
NOLAN. (*From offstage*) No. I got it. It's old. I think it's too old to
eat.
CARISSA. Just cut off the moldy parts.
NOLAN. (*From offstage*) I can do that.

*Nolan comes back out. He has a tiny piece of cheese on a plate.
He also has a bottle of red wine.*

NOLAN. There wasn't much left after I—
CARISSA. That's okay.
NOLAN. You take it.
CARISSA. Are you sure?

NOLAN. Please.

> *Carissa takes the one slice of cheese and eats it slowly, sensually, watching Nolan closely the entire time. She holds **No Way to Win** in the other hand, against her chest. Nolan is mesmerized.*

Um—would you—would you like some—you know, that is a very mediocre book.

CARISSA. I've heard it's good.

NOLAN. Well, the author. That guy. I know him—well, I don't
    know him. My ex is more familiar with him. I believe it's the
    reason she's in New York so much lately.

CARISSA. Wow—now I'll have to read it.

> *Carissa opens the jacket insert and looks at the picture of Felix inside.*

This guy? Come on. Who would leave you for this guy?

NOLAN. That's nice but you don't have to make me feel better. I
    actually don't think she *left* me for him. I think that—

CARISSA. Wine.

NOLAN. What?

> *Noticing that he's holding the bottle.*

Oh right. Wine. It's red.

CARISSA. It is.

> *Nolan pours the wine into the crystal goblets. He's shaking.*

Don't be nervous.

NOLAN. I'm not—no, I'm not nervous at all, really.

CARISSA. Good, 'cause I'm not.

NOLAN. No, you don't seem like the type who would be.

CARISSA. Not because I've done this before.

NOLAN. Oh good. I mean—

CARISSA. I just like you.

NOLAN. Thank you. I like you—so, well. Here's to—uh—to—

CARISSA. To a lazy, blue Sunday.

NOLAN. You just took the words—exactly.

CARISSA. Matches.

NOLAN. Matches—let me—here—I have some somewhere.

CARISSA. You had them in your hand when you pulled out the
        cigarettes.

NOLAN. That's right. Here you go.

Carissa lights a match.

CARISSA. Do you mind?

NOLAN. I don't think so.

Carissa lights the candles on the table.

CARISSA. How long were you married?

NOLAN. Too long. Six years.

CARISSA. (*Laughing*) That's not long. You could live to be ninety.

NOLAN. I can't imagine.

CARISSA. It's like relationships, you know, they have life spans. And
        some last and some die quickly. Six years is nothing. You
        have a lot of good things ahead of you.

NOLAN. I don't know.

CARISSA. No. I'm sure you do. At least you were still in the single
        digits. What's a few years invested? Nothing compared to a

couple decades.

NOLAN. True.

CARISSA. Last night I was lying in bed and I was thinking—you know, I've never had a double digit relationship. It's this whole idea of longevity. I don't know. I'll never get married.

NOLAN. No, don't say that.

CARISSA. I don't want to. I think I'd find it confining, but mainly because it's this thing relationships do. I mean, let's face it, they die. And it's much harder to accept that when you're married to someone. So people stay married and the marriage just becomes this sort of hollow shell.

NOLAN. Empty.

CARISSA. Exactly. I don't understand how people can go through life like that—faking it.

NOLAN. I don't know if this is true but I've heard that for some people it comes back. You know, they lose it and then they somehow get it back.

CARISSA. With the same person? God, that's really optimistic for an accountant.

NOLAN. What do you do?

CARISSA. I paint. I'm an artist.

NOLAN. Really?

CARISSA. Really. Yeah.

NOLAN. I would've guessed that. No, I would've. I mean, that's great—an artist. So, you've pretty much made it? I mean you make a living off it?

CARISSA. Okay, you *are* an accountant.

NOLAN. Sorry.

CARISSA. No, it's okay. I make decent money. In spurts.

NOLAN. I'm so fascinated with that whole thing—you know, that creative thing.

CARISSA. I have two choices—paint or kill myself.

NOLAN. Wow—that's—umm—you take it really seriously.

CARISSA. My ex-boyfriend said I was fanatical. But he didn't understand. He was so demanding. You know, he was jealous. But I thought we could work it out, that he loved me enough to accept all of me. I don't know. I thought Eddie would last. He should've never made it a choice. He's a professor. He's almost tenured and he's living this very structured and organized life and I just didn't fit into it in the long run. Not to diminish—I mean, he's an amazing man—he's brilliant. You'd never know it if you met him on the street. But that's because he's not pretentious. What am I saying? He hated Bergman—the hell with him.

NOLAN. Who's Bergman?

CARISSA. The director.

NOLAN. Oh—*that* Bergman. So what does your ex teach?

CARISSA. Art History. I still think he won't appreciate me until I'm dead. What about your ex?

NOLAN. Sarah? Sarah's alive. It's a long—please don't tell me you ran into her because I can't go through that again.

CARISSA. I'm sure I don't know her.

NOLAN. Okay, good—good because—God—that would be too much, anyway. It's a long story. She met my ex-wife—my other one. And then she left.

CARISSA. What? They compared notes?

NOLAN. Apparently—yes. That's exactly what they did. I have this habit of kicking my dirty underwear under the bed.

CARISSA. No—

NOLAN. Yeah—

CARISSA. No, I do that.

NOLAN. Really?

CARISSA. I swear, I do.

NOLAN. (*Laughing*) What a disaster we'd be together!

> *Beat.*

I mean—

CARISSA. I don't like to wear underwear anyway.

NOLAN. Oh.

CARISSA. I mean—

NOLAN. No, that's okay.

CARISSA. I mean when I sleep—

NOLAN. So right now—

CARISSA. Right now I'm wearing—under—oh my God.

NOLAN. I made you nervous. You have this sort of nice red flush to
      your face.

CARISSA. Oh God—it takes a lot for me to—

NOLAN. It's nice.

CARISSA. How'd we get from dirty underwear to this?

NOLAN. Relationships.

CARISSA. Relationships—yeah.

NOLAN. Single digit relationships.

CARISSA. You know I've never gone into a relationship thinking that
      this one was it. You know, the one that'll last forever so—so
      it's okay for me to be investing this much time and energy—so
      we'll get married and live happily ever after—blah blah blah.

NOLAN. Maybe you never met the right one.

CARISSA. I think they were all the right one—I mean for me, at that
      point in my life, they were right. Eddie was right while Eddie
      was right.

NOLAN. I like that.

Beat. Nolan looks at Carissa like he's going to pounce her.

CARISSA. You know—my car.

NOLAN. Your car? I forgot about your car.

CARISSA. It won't get towed or anything, will it?

NOLAN. Not on a Sunday.

CARISSA. Except I'm sort of blocking that driveway.

NOLAN. I'll check it.

CARISSA. No, that's okay. I can—

NOLAN. I can move it to my driveway—

CARISSA. Oh—

NOLAN. I mean if you want to hang out—

CARISSA. Well, maybe I should just give you my number.

NOLAN. Or—yeah. Whatever.

> *Carissa smiles. She exits offstage. Nolan finishes off his glass of wine and goes to blow out the candles but then decides against it.*

> *Carissa returns.*

CARISSA. Hi. My car is gone.

NOLAN. What? It's gone? What?

CARISSA. My car is not there. It was there. Now it's not there.

NOLAN. You're kidding. Your car's not there?

CARISSA. God damn it. I better use your phone.

NOLAN. They are really quick.

CARISSA. I left my phone in my car.

NOLAN. Use my phone—no, you sit down. I'll call.

> *Nolan begins to exit to the kitchen. He stops.*

Do you think you might want to go out sometime—with me?

CARISSA. Go out?

NOLAN. Or we could stay in.

CARISSA. Right now?

NOLAN. Okay. Sure. I mean right now.

CARISSA. It is Sunday.

NOLAN. It is.

CARISSA. And it is soggy—

NOLAN. Very soggy.

CARISSA. And blue.

NOLAN. Did I tell you how much I love you—blue. How much I love
blue?

Carissa smiles at Nolan. Black out.

.

ACT TWO - SCENE THREE
"EDDIE & WYNNE"

Carissa's studio/loft. Over a year later.

Carissa's studio is almost exactly as it was in Act One. The big canvas isn't done. Now however three abstract paintings of blue hearts are suspended from the ceiling among other staggered hanging frames and blank canvases.

*Tarps are scattered on the ground. Another canvas sits on the easel. A copy of **No Way to Win** is on the floor next to the easel along with various cans of paint of different colors, including red.*

A retro rock song plays loudly on Carissa's stereo but Carissa is nowhere to be found.

Eddie enters the studio cautiously and leaves the door open. He pulls a set of keys out of his pant pocket and sets them on an easel—a difficult moment for him.

Wynne enters behind him and stands back watching him. She goes to the stereo and turns off the music.

Both silently walk through the studio, amongst the canvases and frames, but ultimately Eddie and Wynne end up looking up at the large, unfinished canvas.

WYNNE. Who is she?

EDDIE. Who is who?

WYNNE. This woman.

EDDIE. Carissa?

WYNNE. Who is she to you?

EDDIE. No one. She hasn't been anyone to me for a long time.

WYNNE. But you came here.

EDDIE. To give her back her keys. We can go.

WYNNE. Already? We just got here.

Wynne continues to look around.

You're in love with this artist.

EDDIE. I *was* in love with her.

Wynne is walking in and out of the suspended frames as she talks to Eddie. Occasionally, she stops, looking out through a frame as if she is the picture.

EDDIE. I shouldn't have brought you here.

WYNNE. She's very good. Do you think she's good?

EDDIE. She's good. I guess. It's hard to appreciate the art when you know the artist intimately.

WYNNE. You can't separate it? You can't see it objectively?

EDDIE. I don't want to see it at all, to be honest with you.

WYNNE. The thing you loved about her was also the thing you hated. Maybe she's too good.

EDDIE. Maybe she is. Maybe she was just a pain in the ass.

WYNNE. It's been hard for you without her.

EDDIE. I don't think so.

WYNNE. When did you break up?

EDDIE. I don't know. A year ago. Something like that.

WYNNE. It took you a whole year to drop off her keys?

EDDIE. So what?

WYNNE. You could've mailed them.

EDDIE. I could've. I didn't.

WYNNE. It's okay that you're here. It's a natural impulse. You haven't seen her in a long time. You must wonder what's become of her—wonder if you could be her friend.

EDDIE. We were never friends. On good days, maybe lovers—but there weren't many good days.

WYNNE. She had other lovers?

EDDIE. No.

WYNNE. How do you know?

EDDIE. She didn't have time for other lovers. She didn't have time for me.

WYNNE. I see.

EDDIE. She cares about one thing.

WYNNE. Herself?

EDDIE. Her work.

> *Wynne floats to the canvas at the back of the studio, closer to Eddie.*

WYNNE. Her work is herself, isn't it? Like this blue heart she's painting.

> *Beat. Eddie looks at the canvas. Then he looks at the other canvases hanging around him.*

EDDIE. She's doing a series.

> *He touches the canvas.*

WYNNE. She seems very content.

EDDIE. Carissa content? Highly unlikely.

WYNNE. Compensating then. Trying to find balance.

EDDIE. Without medication? I don't think so.

WYNNE. She's unstable?

EDDIE. No, it was our relationship that was unstable.

WYNNE. She was the brilliant one and you were—

EDDIE. Nothing.

WYNNE. Nothing?

Eddie looks around the studio.

EDDIE. On to yet another shade of blue. Broadening her palette.
　　　　Redundant, but why not. So is love. Of course, for her it's
　　　　easily reduced to benign symbols and colors.

WYNNE. Simplified, but limited.

EDDIE. Very much so.

WYNNE. I see why it didn't work out for you two.

EDDIE. Why is that?

WYNNE. You couldn't help but be her critic. It's what you do.

EDDIE. But I wasn't—

WYNNE. Perfect love is clear.

Beat.

EDDIE. I thought so, too. But she said that was impossible. Love like
　　　　that would be too simple. I guess it's all subjective.

WYNNE. Is it? Is love?

Wynne bends down, dipping a paintbrush in a can of red paint.

WYNNE. Do you think hearts should be red?

*Wynne, still squatted down by the can of red paint, notices the
copy of No Way to Win on the tarp. She grabs the book and*

opens it.

EDDIE. Careful with that—you'll drip it—

    Eddie takes the paintbrush from Wynne.

No. I don't think love is red. Not that I would mind if it was.

    He looks at the canvas and then back at the brush dipped in red paint.

WYNNE. I said *hearts.*
EDDIE. What?
WYNNE. Do you think *hearts* should be red?
EDDIE. Hearts can be blue. Whatever.
WYNNE. Blood is blue in your veins.
EDDIE. Carissa isn't that literal. Blue is for—for other reasons.
WYNNE. Like what?
EDDIE. I don't know. She had reasons.
WYNNE. (*Looking at the book*) Who is Nolan?
EDDIE. Nolan? I have no idea.
WYNNE. He gave her this book. It says right here in the front.
    (*She reads*) To Carissa, with all my love like blue. Nolan.

    Eddie takes the paintbrush and makes a large bold red stroke across the big canvas.

Look what you did.

    Eddie continues painting red over one of Carissa's paintings.

EDDIE. (*Painting*) I take red, I put it over blue and it comes out a purplish color. A little more red—look—

Wynne moves away from him as she looks through the book.

A little more purple. All through history people have associated purple with—with something. From here on out, purple will be the color of love.

Realizing she's not watching.

Where did you go?

Wynne is standing behind a suspended frame. She reads to herself from the book.

WYNNE. What?
EDDIE. Purple is now the color of love.
WYNNE. You better take that painting home with you.
EDDIE. I'd rather leave it here—as a gift.
WYNNE. She's in love with Nolan now. I don't think she'll care.
EDDIE. She'll care. I've desecrated her shrine.
WYNNE. I can think of a better way to desecrate it.
EDDIE. What did you say?

Wynne laughs.

WYNNE. Do I have to call you Professor Mitchell if we're not at school?
EDDIE. I prefer Eddie—as long as we're not at school.
WYNNE. You wanted her to be here.
EDDIE. No. I really didn't.
WYNNE. This is where you were on that last night.

EDDIE. How do you know that?

WYNNE. Because you're here now. It's like returning to the scene of the crime. People do it all the time when they lose love. They go back and try to find it again—like it got tossed under the couch or a rug or maybe it's at the bottom of a can of red paint. People think love is a thing they can retrieve at will.

EDDIE. You've never been in love?

WYNNE. I don't know what that is—I know when I need to rest—

EDDIE. And what you call rest? That's not some sort of attachment?

WYNNE. No, it's rest.

EDDIE. So men are rest stops for you? Is that what I am?

> *Wynne clutches the book to her chest tightly. She doesn't answer.*

I guess it doesn't matter.

> *Beat.*

I try not to notice students.

WYNNE. I try not to be noticed.

EDDIE. There was something about you.

WYNNE. Well, you seemed lonely and sad.

EDDIE. And you seemed interesting but aloof.

WYNNE. You think I'm interesting?

EDDIE. And aloof. Which makes it impossible to—

WYNNE. To what?

EDDIE. To get involved. I don't get involved with students—

WYNNE. Was she a student?

EDDIE. No. She was teaching part-time.

WYNNE. I'll drop your class.

EDDIE. Am I that boring?

WYNNE. We're both adults. There's no law.

EDDIE. We should wait until the course ends.

WYNNE. (*Laughs*) I don't know if I'll be in the mood then. But thank you.

EDDIE. What am I doing? I should not have brought you here.

WYNNE. You didn't want to come alone. I understand. And if she were here—it would look better to have someone with you.

EDDIE. That's not it. I like being with you but—

WYNNE. But what? I'm not jail bait.

Beat.

I get it.

Wynne turns to walk out. She still has the book.

EDDIE. Wynne, you can't take the book.

WYNNE. I'd like to keep it.

EDDIE. That's stealing.

WYNNE. And what about your art work? What's that?

EDDIE. I would call it destructive collaboration.

WYNNE. Fancy words for vandalism.

EDDIE. I feel like I have the right to do this. For what I gave—

WYNNE. I feel like I have a right to take this book then.

EDDIE. That's crazy. You don't have anything to do with this.

WYNNE. This book—it's about me.

EDDIE. What do you mean?

WYNNE. I mean it's based on me.

EDDIE. What do you mean—it's based on you?

WYNNE. Just what I said. I lived with the author when I was in New York City and he wrote this book about me.

EDDIE. (*not believing*) Come on.

WYNNE. It's not really about me. It's about him—about him trying to figure me out.

EDDIE. You must be quite an enigma.

WYNNE. Only if you need to over think things.

EDDIE. What is the book?

WYNNE. *No Way to Win.* Get it?

EDDIE. No way to *you.* Nice.

WYNNE. See, you're quick. I like men who are quick. It saves so
much time.

EDDIE. I'll have to read that book.

WYNNE. Why? I'm right here.

EDDIE. Then we might as well leave this copy.

Eddie takes the book out of her hands.

I don't know why she has this. In all the years we were
together, she never read much.

WYNNE. People change.

EDDIE. They do?

WYNNE. Will you read it to me?

Eddie looks around with some nervousness.

Please.

Eddie opens the book to the front.

Not there. I left before he finished the ending. I'd like to know
how it ends.

*Eddie turns to the end of **No Way to Win**.*

EDDIE. (*Reading*) It's a hell of an idea—Love—and I'm glad we came
up with it. As sure as it entropies, it reconstructs itself,
regenerates and reinvents itself. There is a guarantee after all.
Chaos will turn to order then to chaos again and back to a new

order in a miraculous dance of dissipation and discovery. Even in the unions that last a lifetime. Dissolution and discovery. We're connected whether we like it or not. The dance itself never ends. And in the stillness between letting go and touching for the first time—the lag between loss and gain—I learn, I grow, I change. I prepare to love again. Better than before.

Eddie closes the book.

Wynne kisses Eddie gently on the cheek. She takes the book from his hands and holds it for a minute. She sets it down on a tarp.

Wynne goes to leave. She looks back to see Eddie standing at the big painting.

WYNNE. She was making it for you.
EDDIE. How do you know?
WYNNE. I just do.

Wynne exits. Eddie, now alone, looks up at the large canvas for a couple beats.

EDDIE. (*calling to Wynne*) Hey wait up.

Eddie leaves the studio to catch up with Wynne.

Black Out. The End.

About the Playwright

Kristen Lazarian is an award-winning playwright who has had her full-length and short plays produced, work-shopped and stage-read at many venues in L.A. including the Geffen Playhouse, Theatre 40, East-West Players, Theatre Geo, the Road Theatre, Pacific Resident Theatre, 68 Cent Crew, and the Blank Theatre. Her plays have also been staged across the United States, including New York City. She has had productions internationally in Holland, England, Australia, and Canada. Her plays include *Push, Love Like Blue, Flesh & Tenderness, Inviting Karma, Sophisticated Barflies & Other Short Plays*, and more.

In addition to writing plays, Kristen is a screenwriter. She penned the Hay House film, *The Shift*, based on the spiritual teachings of self-improvement pioneer Wayne Dyer. She currently works as a writer and script consultant on various projects and has works in development.

Kristen is a member of the Dramatist Guild and the Alliance of Los Angeles Playwrights. She lives in Los Angeles with her husband and their three sons.

What people are saying about

LOVE LIKE BLUE

"One of the reasons that **Love Like Blue** works so well is its brilliantly original concept.... as playwright Lazarian has created six very real, imperfect, intriguing, and human characters. Lazarian's dialogue is so good, so real, so natural..." *StageSceneLA*

"Beautifully written, with finely tuned skill, heartfelt passion, and universally relatable humor – a must see." *Tolucan Times*

"Lazarian's play has a marvelously neat structure that complements her prickly observations on love and relationships." *Studio City Sun*

"... a hearfelt and compelling play by the award-winning Kristen Lazarian... You know when a play is good when it sends you home thinking." *LA Splash*

"Loved it, loved it, loved it! A must see – the writing was brilliant... could really relate to many of the emotions and experiences depicted through out." *LA Times Calendar Live*

A unanimous RAVE at *Los Angeles Times* Calendar Live!

Also by Kristen Lazarian

full length plays:

Push

Flesh & Tenderness

Inviting Karma

Grace

Between You & Me

short plays:

Sophisticated Barflies

Joy Ride

The Other Side of Meaning

Recovery

Beach Balls

So Nice To See You

Intimate Distances

Angel in the Attic

In the Church of the Pen

Spring Forgets

Imaginings

Bad News

My Name is Bridget

Harry & the Witch

Slow Burn

www.ingramcontent.com/pod-product-compliance
Lightning Source LLC
Chambersburg PA
CBHW030540180626
46810CB00005B/1946